*For Edward William Hartwell and Charlie Alber Backes. Enjoy the Ride. — P.J.*

*For Rose, Finn and Nandi — B.G.*

Text copyright © 2019 by Pamela Jane
Illustrations copyright © 2019 by Barry Gott

Publisher's Cataloging-in-Publication Data

Names: Jane, Pamela, author. | Gott, Barry, illustrator.
Title: Trucks zooming by / by Pamela Jane ; illustrated by Barry Gott.
Description: New York, NY: Starberry Books, an imprint of Kane Press, Inc., 2019.
Summary: A young girl lives out her dream of riding in her family's truck for the day.
Identifiers: LCCN 2018965804 | ISBN 9781635921304 (Hardcover) | 9781635921311 (ebook)
Subjects: LCSH Trucks--Juvenile fiction. | Family--Juvenile fiction. | CYAC Trucks--Fiction. |
Family--Fiction. | BISAC JUVENILE FICTION / Transportation / Cars & Trucks
Classification: LCC PZ7.J213 Tru 2019 | DDC [E]--dc23

Library of Congress Control Number: 2018965804

10 9 8 7 6 5 4 3 2 1

First published in the United States of America in 2019 by StarBerry Books, an imprint of Kane Press, Inc.

Printed in China

StarBerry Books is a registered trademark of Kane Press, Inc.

Book Design: Joan M. McEvoy

Visit us online at www.kanepress.com

Like us on Facebook facebook.com/kanepress

Follow us on Twitter @KanePress

# Trucks Zooming By

🍓 StarBerry Books
**New York**

It's time to get up now.
We're ready to load.

Goodbye to the city.
Hello to the road!

We roll down the highway,
Beneath the bright sky

While I keep a lookout
For trucks zooming by.

Trash trucks and tow trucks
Go clickety-clack.

That red fire engine
Has dogs in the back.

Drill trucks with ladders
And long rubber hoses,

Trailers with horses
That stick out their noses!

Dump trucks and diggers
And farm trucks for hogs,

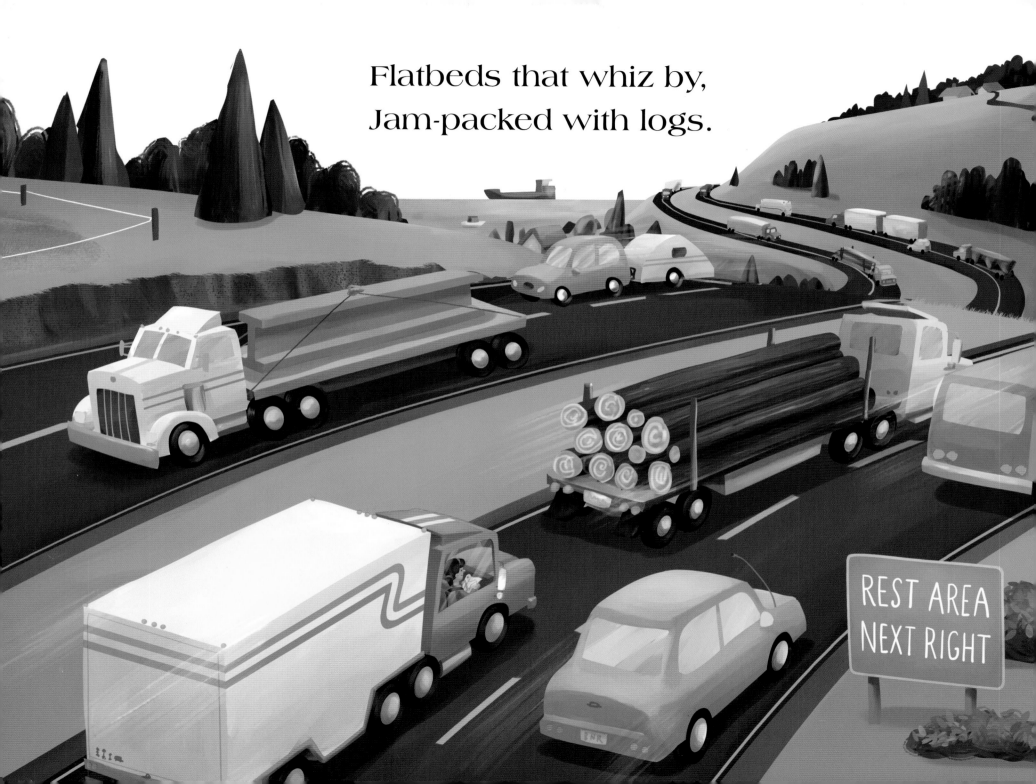

Flatbeds that whiz by,
Jam-packed with logs.

REST AREA
NEXT RIGHT

Panels and pickups,
Red, yellow, and blue,

Cart stuff to the coast
And back again, too.

Whatever needs hauling,
From pizza to pigs,

Can ride right along
On those fabulous rigs!

A trucker will haul things

A very short way

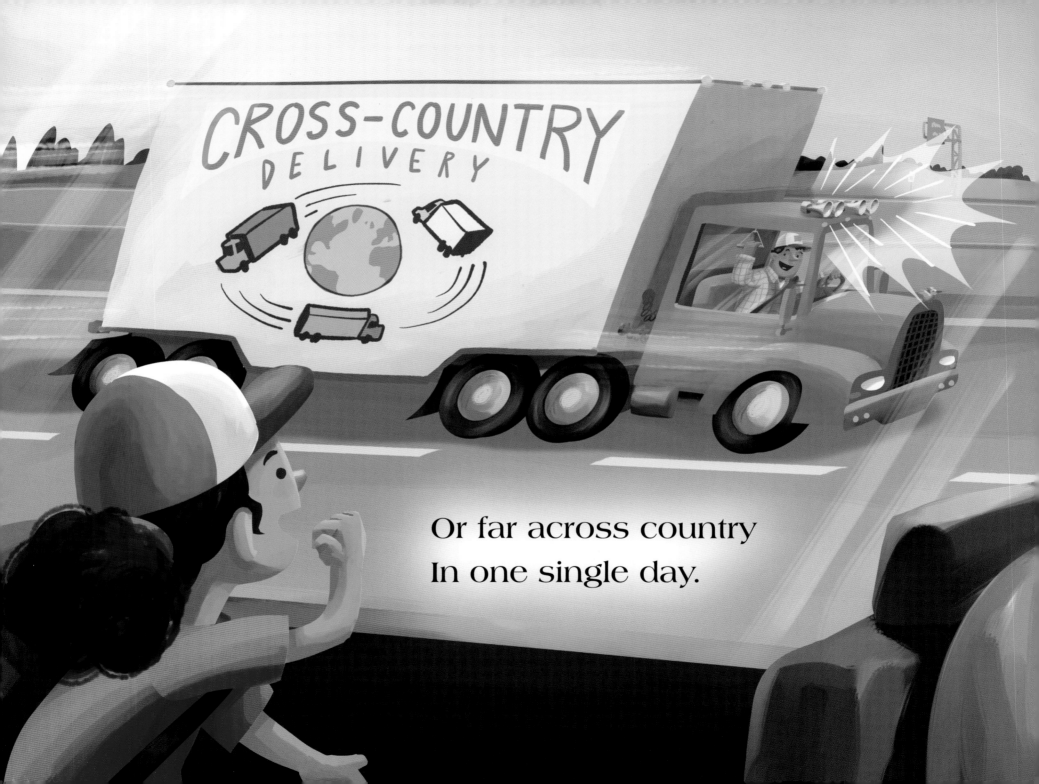

Or far across country
In one single day.

We roll off the highway,
Beneath the night sky.

I take one last look
At the trucks zooming by.

Someday when I'm older,
If I have any luck,

I'll make enough money
To buy my own truck.

But till that time comes
I'm just really glad

I can ride in a truck
With my mom and my dad!

# Can you find all of these trucks in the book?

## A TRASH TRUCK

is used for collecting trash. It picks up garbage from bins outside homes or from dumpsters outside large buildings. Once the trash is dumped into the truck, a moving plate is used to crush it. This makes room for more garbage in the truck. Your neighborhood trash truck can carry about 50,000 pounds of trash!

## A TOW TRUCK

is a vehicle built for moving cars or other trucks that have broken down. It's designed with special equipment that can pull a heavy vehicle over long distances. When a car breaks down, a tow truck will come to the rescue. Large tow trucks can tow up to 50,000 pounds.

## A FOOD TRUCK

is designed for selling food. It may have an oven, a sink, and a fridge inside. Food trucks sell everything from tacos to pizzas to falafel to ice cream. A food truck is really a restaurant on wheels!

## A DUMP TRUCK

is often used at construction sites to haul heavy things like bricks, sand, or salt. It's called a dump truck because its back end opens and lifts so that whatever is being carried can be dumped out. A dump truck can hold about 50,000 pounds of material!

## A DIGGER

has a bucket to scoop up heavy loads of dirt, gravel, or even snow. Diggers don't have regular wheels. They roll along on rotating tracks. The largest diggers weigh as much as 195 elephants and can do the job of 20 people with shovels!

## A FLATBED TRUCK

has no sides or roof, only an open, flat surface. Flatbeds are good for carrying large and heavy equipment. Because they don't have a roof, it's possible for the trucks to carry objects of any size.

## A DRILL TRUCK

is made for drilling deep below the surface of the earth. Drill trucks can drill wells for oil or water and can even make tunnels through mountains. These trucks can drill 10 miles into the earth's crust and stand as tall as 150 feet!

## A TRAILER

is built for transporting animals such as horses. Trailers come in many sizes, with some carrying two horses and others carrying ten. Thick, heavy floor mats make the ride more comfortable for the animals. And hay bags are often brought along so the horses can have a snack on their road trip.

## A FIRE ENGINE

is built for taking firefighters to a fire. It carries special equipment for fighting fires, like water pumps, hoses, ladders, and first-aid equipment. Why are fire engines always red? No one knows for sure, but the bright color helps them stand out from other vehicles on the road.

## A PANEL TRUCK

is used to deliver things like construction materials, food, furniture, packages—and many other items. Some panel trucks have an opening in back for farmers to sell their goods. The truck becomes a portable fruit and vegetable stand!

## A PICKUP TRUCK

is one of the most common trucks on the road. Having an open back with sides allows it to easily carry things like firewood, building materials, or small equipment. In fact, you can transport just about anything in pickup trucks. They're so useful that some people even use them as their family car!

## A TANKER TRUCK

is used to transport liquids like gasoline, milk, or even dangerous chemicals. Large tankers that carry milk are refrigerated and can hold up to 8,000 gallons at one time!